Krishna's

Butter Bash

by

ini Supriyananda

as narrated by

ui Swaroopananda

C·H·I·N·M·A·Y·A   B·A·L·A   K·A·T·H·A

Early one morning, as the sun was just rising and the birds began chirping, Krishna woke up from a long and wonderful sleep. He tossed off his blanket, hopped out of bed and stretched out his chubby little arms.

Krishna was a little boy with chubby cheeks, a round face and soft blue skin. He was very cute, and very witty, and very VERY mischievous.

Everyone loved him. Everyone really loved him.

He looked out of his window and thought, "It's a nice day." He smiled to himself and thought "...a nice day to get up to some mischief!" He giggled.

Then he saw some monkeys. They were also just waking up. Krishna grinned a mischievous little grin, with a naughty look in his big brown eyes. He waved his playful little hands at them. The monkeys would help him carry out his mischievous plans for the day, he was sure.

Krishna lived in a beautiful town called Gokul. All the ladies in the town were called Gopies. And all the young boys, who were Krishna's friends, were called Gopa Balas. The Gopies and Gopas spent their days looking after the mother cows and baby calves.

So Krishna and his friends set off as usual, taking the calves out to graze in the open fields on this beautiful, beautiful morning. While the cows chewed and chewed on the luscious green grass, Krishna and his friends played games.

After a while, one of Krishna's friends tapped him on the shoulder and said, "Krishna, I'm hungry." Another friend said, "Me, too!" Soon all his friends were complaining, "We're so hungry!" Krishna was hungry, too.

Krishna loved butter. He REALLY loved butter.

The Gopies made butter from fresh cow's milk. They made the butter so yummy, it tasted like ice-cream.

Krishna was dreaming of butter. He went and said, "Gopi Aunty! Gopi Aunty! Can you give me some butter?" The Gopies loved this sweet little boy and wanted to keep him with them.

So they said, "Not unless you sing for us." So Krishna sang. The Gopies gave him a tiny little bit of butter.

Krishna wanted more. But the Gopies said, "Not unless you dance for us." So Krishna danced. Again the Gopies gave him a tiny little bit of butter.

But Krishna wanted some more. "Not unless you play the flute for us," said the Gopies. So Krishna played his magical flute. But the Gopies only gave him a tiny little bit of butter.

Krishna was not happy. He sang, he danced, he played his flute, but they gave him so little butter.

"This is not fair," he thought. "They have so much butter, and they are giving me so little, even after making me do so much."

Krishna went back to his friends.

"Did you bring us any butter?" asked the Gopa Balas. "No," said Krishna, "they didn't give enough even for me." "Oh, but we are so hungry!" said his friends again.

Suddenly Krishna smiled an extra naughty smile, his big eyes became even bigger, and he chuckled a really mischievous chuckle. "Let's go steal some butter!" said Krishna.

"What? STEAL butter?" said his friends.

Krishna sneaked back to the village. All his friends carefully, quietly followed him. He looked around to make sure no one was watching, and then ran towards a house.

Standing on his tippy toes, he peeked through the window to check if anyone was home. Nobody was.

So he got the biggest boy in the group to bend over, then climbed on his back and jumped through the window.

His friends all followed him in. *Plonk, plonk, plonk,* they fell on top of each other as they came through the window.

They found a big pot of butter and dug in. There was so much butter, enough for everyone and more. Krishna looked out the window and saw the monkeys swinging on the trees. He whistled to them to come in.

The monkeys jumped through the window. *Plonk, plonk, plonk,* they fell on top of each other. Krishna fed butter to the monkeys, and it got all over their faces.

The boys and the monkeys had butter everywhere. There was butter on their hands, butter on their mouths, butter in their hair, butter even on the monkeys' tails. There was butter on the floor, on the door, on the stove and on all the boys' nice bright-coloured clothes.

They used the butter to slip and slide. They held onto the tails of the monkeys and went for a fun ride. *Zwing......!!!!*

What a grand butter party they had.

They had butter to eat, butter to share and butter to play with. They giggled, they chuckled, and they laughed. What fun! What fun!

When the Gopies came home that day, ai-ya!, they found such a mess. The pots were broken and the butter was stolen. "Who could have done this? Who is the butter thief?" they shouted.

Do you know who?
Shhh!

Do you want Krishna to get caught?

Nobody wanted Krishna to get caught, so nobody told anybody, but everybody asked somebody.

The Gopies had an idea. They knew how to trick the butter thief. They found a place for the butter where it was very safe. Very safe, indeed.

The next day Krishna and his friends again sneaked into the house. They looked for the butter. They searched and searched. They looked in the drawer, they looked under the bed, and they looked in all the cupboards. They could not find it. Where could it be?

Until one little boy saw the butterpot hanging from the ceiling. "Oh, no! Now how will we get the butter? It's too high!" the little boy cried.

"Don't worry," said Krishna. **"If you think calmly, there is always a way."** Krishna looked at all his friends and said, "Now let us think." So they put their chins in the palm of their hands, their arms folded tightly, and they all looked up at the pot. "How.... How.... How...?"

Suddenly Krishna jumped up. Krishna smiled an extra naughty smile, his big eyes become even bigger, and he chuckled a really mischievous chuckle. "We'll make a human pyramid," said the blue boy.

So the bigger boys formed the base, the smaller boys climbed on top of the bigger boys, and the still smaller boys climbed on top of the other small boys. And Krishna climbed on top of them all.

He stretched out his chubby little arms and caught hold of the butterpot. *Oops!* He pulled it too hard and all the boys tumbled on top of each other. Krishna fell on top of them, with the butterpot right in his hands.

They giggled, and chuckled, and laughed. Once again they had a big grand butter party.

The Gopies came home and, *ai-ya-yah!*, again found a big mess. "Oh dear!" said the astonished Gopies. "The butter thief is huge. He can reach the ceiling. Maybe.... maybe... maybe he's a giant!" They shuddered.

Everybody asked somebody, "Who is the butter thief?" But nobody told anybody. They thought it was a big and wild butter-monster. They didn't know it was actually lovable little Krishna.

But you know, don't you? *Shhh!* Don't tell! You don't want Krishna to get caught, do you?

Every day Krishna and his friends would sneak in to an empty house in the village and steal butter. Every day they would have a grand butter party. Each day the monkeys would join them.

And every day they would make a big mess!

One such day, just as Krishna got to the very top of the human pyramid, and stretched out his chubby little arms to reach for the butterpot, the front door opened and in walked a big Gopi.

She saw Krishna and the boys and the monkeys and she shrieked, "*Eeeeek!* What are you all doing?"

"*AAAHHHHH!*" went Krishna's friends.

Everyone got so frightened and the human pyramid fell. All the little boys and monkeys ran everywhere. Some ran here, others ran there. Some jumped out the window, others ran through the door.

The big Gopi gave chase, running here and there to catch the naughty butter thieves, but they were too fast for her. All the little boys and monkeys escaped. Finally, completely and extremely exhausted, she stopped to catch her breath.

She stood in the middle of the room with her hands on her hips, and slowly looked up at the butterpot. Who was left hanging up there alone?

Krishna!

Krishna was still holding onto the butterpot as it hung from the ceiling. *Swing, swing....* it swayed from side to side, and Krishna swayed with it.

The Gopi gave Krishna a very angry look, but Krishna looked back at her very innocently with his big sweet brown eyes.

The Gopi's heart was now melting. And so was the butter in Krishna's hands, which slipped from the pot

Down Krishna fell, *plonk!*
Right on top of Gopi Aunty.

They both fell to the floor with a big loud *thud*.

The Gopi quickly caught hold of Krishna's soft chubby hands and said, "*A-hah!* So you're the butter thief! Now I've caught you butter-handed."

"I'm going to take you to your mother. The whole town will know who the butter thief is. You sneak into our houses, break our pots, steal our butter, and make a big mess!" said Gopi Aunty quite firmly.

The Gopi took Krishna by the hand and started walking towards Krishna's house.

Krishna had to do something, quick!

As they were walking, suddenly Krishna smiled an extra naughty smile, his big eyes become even bigger, and he softly chuckled a really mischievous chuckle.

Krishna saw some children playing in the distance. Among them was Gopi Aunty's little son. He was Krishna's friend.

Krishna waved as if to say *'Hi'*, then signalled to him to come closer.

The Gopi's son with his eyes questioned Krishna, "What happened?" Krishna replied gesturing to the little boy to come and help him. Carefully, quietly, the two friends came up with a secret wonderful plan.

Krishna tickled the Gopi's hand, so she laughed and let go for just a second. Quickly Krishna pulled out his hand, and suddenly, the Gopi's son was holding his mother's hand. The Gopi did not realize what had happened.

Krishna raced through the backstreet towards his house. He ran as fast as his little legs could take him. He wiped all the butter out of his hands and around his mouth, and sat down pretending to do his homework.

Soon the big Gopi knocked on Krishna's door and called out to Krishna's mother, "Yashoda, open up! I have caught your naughty little son stealing butter."

Mother Yashoda opened the door, surprised, and said, "My son STEALING?"

"Yes," said the big Gopi quite firmly. "I have found him in my house butter-handed."

Mother Yashoda looked down at the little boy whose hand the Gopi was holding, and started laughing.

The Gopi was shocked. "I have brought Krishna to be punished, and his mother is laughing," she thought. She looked down at Krishna, BUT... .

"But...... what?.......how?....er....."

"Where was Krishna?" The Gopi was holding her own little son's hand. She was stunned.

Krishna appeared from behind Mother Yashoda. He tilted his head, and grinning an impish little grin, with a naughty look in his big brown eyes, he waved his playful little hands."Hi, Gopi Aunty," he said.

"You naughty boy, why did you steal the butter?" said the Gopi Anuty.

"Me! Steal?" said Krishna, "why would I steal? There is so much butter in my house."

"That's right," said Mother Yashoda, "I have so much butter for my dear little Krishna, he can eat all day long. Why would he steal butter from you?"

Do you know? Why does Krishna 'steal' butter?

Because...... .

Actually, **the Gopies loved Krishna.**

They adored Krishna. They dreamt of him all day long. They wanted Krishna in their homes. They wanted him to eat their butter.

Do you know what the Gopies did when they woke up in the morning?

They would say, **"Krishna, Krishna!"**

In their hearts all day long, "Krishna, Krishna! Krishna, Krishna!"

When they took their bath, "Krishna, Krishna!"
When they washed the cows, "Krishna, Krishna!"
When they fed the cows, "Krishna, Krishna!"
When they milked the cows, "Krishna, Krishna!"
When they gathered the milk, "Krishna, Krishna!"
When they heated the milk, "Krishna, Krishna!"
When they churned the milk, "Krishna, Krishna!"
When they made the butter, "Krishna, Krishna!"
When they put it into pots, "Krishna, Krishna!"
When they hung up the pots, "Krishna, Krishna!"

In their hearts all day long, "Krishna, Krishna! Krishna, Krishna!"

So whom does the butter belong to?

KRISHNA.

You cannot steal what is already yours. But Krishna did steal something.

He stole their hearts!

Has he stolen yours?

If you want him to, you know what to do.

When you wake up in the morning, "Krishna Krishna!" When you brush your teeth...